Wyatt Walker Turbo Talker

March 2005
Enjoy Wyatt!
Chatter On...
Christine Gormican Hierl

By Christine Gormican Hierl and Michelle Gormican Thompson

Illustrations by Janet M. Thompson

Design by Jennifer L. Smith

Cedar Shamrock Publishing ❃ Madison, Wisconsin

CEDAR SHAMROCK
PUBLISHING

All the Best!
Michelle Gormican Thompson

Printed in the United States of America
By Walsworth Publishing Company

First edition 2004

Cedar Shamrock Publishing
P.O. Box 70775
Madison, WI 53707

ISBN 0-9760680-0-1
Library of Congress Control Number: 2004096395

Cover design and page layout by Jennifer L. Smith

The text of this book is set in Cochin. Georges Peignot designed Cochin based on copper
engravings of the 18th century and Charles Malin cut the typeface in 1912 for the Paris foundry Deberny & Peignot.
The font is named after the French engraver Charles Nicolas Cochin (1715-1790) although its style
had little to do with that of the copper artist's. The font displays a curious mix of style elements and could be placed as
a part of the typographical neorenaissance movement. Cochin is especially large and wide and
was especially popular at the beginning of the 20th century (*www.myfonts.com*).

The original illustrations are in watercolor and watercolor marker.

To my husband Jim and to my sons John and Michael,
who make every day extraordinary.

–CGH

To my husband Craig and my beautiful Bridget Mary
and Joseph Byrnes-you are my life.

–MGT

To Mom and Dad for your love and support.
You gave us the world.

–C & M

In loving memory of my mom,
Alice E. Finsen.

–JT

Meet Wyatt Walker
Turbo Talker
Day and night
Every day
There isn't much he will not say

Wyatt chatters on
His questions fly
Like sparkling fireworks
From the sky

Why do hiccups make me hic?
Can I reach the clouds on my pogo stick?

Why does popcorn have a crunch?
What do babies eat for lunch?

Wyatt chatters on
His words pour out
Like cherry soda
From a fountain spout

Can I pet a polar bear?
Why does Grandma have blue hair?

Can my hamster swim in the kitchen sink?

After the game, what makes my sweaty socks stink?

WHY NOT ?

HOW COME ? CAN I ?

Wyatt chatters on
Like a speeding train
His words spill down
Like pouring rain

Are monkeys good at jumping rope?
When elephants wash, do they use soap?

Is yes the opposite of no?
On cold, cold days, do elves make snow?

Wyatt chatters on
His questions twirl
Like a spinning top
Or a dancing girl

Is the hokey pokey really a dance?
Who put the swish in my corduroy pants?

Why do my eyelashes flitter and flutter?
If I shake up a cow, can I make butter?

He's Wyatt Walker
Turbo Talker
Day and night
Every day
There isn't much he will not say

Wyatt
Walker
Turbo
Talker

When nighttime comes in Wyatt's room
He bids goodnight to the stars and moon

Instead of counting sheep in bed
Wyatt talks himself to sleep instead

The End

About the Authors, Illustrator and Designer

Christine M. Gormican Hierl

Christine is the dean of admissions for a national university. A native of Fond du Lac, Wisconsin, Christine lives in Chicago with her husband Jim and their sons John and Michael.

Michelle L. Gormican Thompson

Michelle is a self-employed public relations consultant. A native of Fond du Lac, Wisconsin, Michelle and her husband Craig live in Madison, Wisconsin with their two kids, Bridget and Joseph. Together with their cousins John and Michael, the foursome's incessant, non-stop and out-of-breath chatter became the inspiration for this book.

Janet M. Thompson

A lifelong commercial and fine artist, Janet lives in Racine, Wisconsin with her husband Ted. Together, they have three sons and seven grandchildren.

Jennifer L. Smith

Jennifer is the managing editor for a governmental association publication. She is also a freelance designer and occasionally writes dance reviews. She lives in Monona, Wisconsin with Kurtis Bock and their German Shepherd, Beowulf.

Special Thanks

The authors would like to extend their gratitude to those individuals who helped make this book a reality.

Wyatt Walker Turbo Talker would not have been possible without the unbelievably beautiful artwork of Janet Thompson. She brought our little friend to life.

Jennifer Smith designed this book and led us through the print process. She is an amazing woman and we feel lucky to know her.

We would also like to thank Erin Fassbender for her design of the Cedar Shamrock logo and Dr. John Gibbons, Dean of Academic Affairs for DeVry University, for his expertise with the editing pen.

Finally, thanks to our Wyatt Walker, who taught us in so many ways that we are truly blessed.

For more information on ordering
Wyatt Walker Turbo Talker
contact:

Cedar Shamrock Publishing
P.O. Box 70775
Madison, WI 53707

Or visit us on the web at
www.wyattwalker.com

CEDAR SHAMROCK
PUBLISHING